PADDINGTON'S LUCKY DAY

For older children Michael Bond has
written nine Paddington story books,
all illustrated by Peggy Fortnum

CIP data may be found at the end of the book.

Paddington's Lucky Day

MICHAEL BOND AND FRED BANBERY

Random House

New York

First American Edition 1974. Text Copyright © 1973 by Michael Bond.
Illustrations Copyright © 1973 by Fred Banbery.
All rights reserved under International and Pan-American Copyright Conventions.
Published in the United States by Random House, Inc., New York.
Originally published in Great Britain as *Paddington Goes Shopping*
by William Collins Sons & Co., Ltd., London.
Manufactured in the United States of America

One day, not long after Paddington went to live
with the Browns at number thirty-two Windsor
Gardens, Mrs. Brown thought she would take
him out shopping.

"We're going to the Portobello Road," explained
Judy. "It's a big outdoor market quite near here."

"You should bring your pocket money," added
Jonathan. "There's a lot to see."

Paddington didn't need asking twice and soon
afterward they all set off.

Suddenly they turned a corner and he found
himself in what seemed like a different world: a

world of outdoor stands and pushcarts, gold and silver ornaments, books, old furniture, fruit and vegetables, people —— His eyes grew larger and larger as he tried to take it all in.

One store was even having its picture taken.
"That's a new supermarket," explained Judy.
"There must be something special going on."
Paddington's mouth began to water as he

peered through the glass. "Perhaps I could do some shopping for you, Mrs. Brown?" he said hopefully.

Mrs. Brown hesitated. She wasn't at all sure about letting him go off on his own quite so soon, but Jonathan told her not to worry.

"Even Paddington can't get lost in a supermarket," he said. "What goes in must come out."

"We can meet him by the check-out counter
on our way back," added Judy.

Paddington felt most important as he entered the store.

He lifted his hat to the manager, who was standing just inside the door, and then consulted Mrs. Brown's shopping list.

Everywhere he looked there were shelves
piled high with boxes and cans. There was
even one shelf with nothing but marmalade.
He could certainly see why it was called
a *super*market.

His paws were soon full and he was just
beginning to wish he'd left his suitcase at home
when he saw the manager coming toward him
pushing a large basket on wheels.

"May I suggest you use one of these, sir?"
he called.

"You can take as much as you want now," he continued.

"Can I really?" exclaimed Paddington.

The manager nodded. "Yes, we like to make

our customers happy."

Paddington looked most impressed. "In that case," he said, "I think I'll have *two* baskets—just to make sure."

The more Paddington saw of the supermarket the more he liked it, and he felt sure Mrs. Brown would be pleased when she saw all her free groceries.

The other customers looked on in amazement.
"Perhaps he's trying to win an eating prize,"
suggested one lady as he went past, his baskets
laden with goods.

But the customers weren't the only ones who were watching Paddington with interest.

Since he had been in the store the manager had been joined by several other important-looking men, and as Paddington reached the check-out counter one of them gave a signal, and they all started to clap.

Paddington had never been in a store where they tried so hard to make their customers happy, and he gave the men a friendly wave as he unloaded his baskets.

"Well done!" said the lady, handing him a ticket. "I hope you've brought a truck with you. There's over a hundred and fifty dollars' worth here!"

Paddington stared at the long roll of paper
in his paw.

"Over a hundred and fifty dollars' worth!" he
gasped, hardly able to believe his eyes or his ears.

Giving the man who had said he could take as
much as he wanted one of his hardest stares,
he opened his suitcase and peered inside.

"But I've only got a nickel!"

Looking up, Paddington suddenly caught
sight of a crowd of people coming toward him.
"Watch out!" cried the lady as he made a
grab for his groceries.
But it was too late. With a roar like an express
train everything began to tumble down off the
counter.

Paddington was still sitting on the floor, covered with groceries, when the Browns rushed into the store to see what was going on.

All in all he decided he was much safer where he was for the time being.

"You wouldn't think," said the manager, "that giving someone a prize would be so difficult."

"A *prize*?" echoed the Browns. The manager pointed to a large notice on the wall.

"This young bear," he said, "happens to be our thousandth customer today. Perhaps you'd like to tell him he's won a free supply of groceries!"

"All of which," said Judy, as they staggered home laden with groceries, "only goes to show that bears always fall on their feet."

"Even in supermarkets!" agreed Jonathan.

Paddington sniffed the air happily. "I like the Portobello Road," he said. "I think I shall always do my shopping here from now on."